Everyday Weapons

Short Stories

Silas Dakar

Copyright © 2025 by Silas Dakar

All rights reserved. No part of this publication may be reproduced, distributed, or transmitted in any form or by any means, including photocopying, recording, or other electronic or mechanical methods, without the prior written permission of the author, except in the case of brief quotations embodied in critical reviews and certain other noncommercial uses permitted by copyright law. For permission requests, write to the author at the email provided below:

Email: **info@silasdakar.com**

This book is published by Silas Dakar and and printed through this publishing house. For more information, visit: **www.silasdakar.com**

Dedication

To my daughters,
May you never lose the strength
to keep moving forward,
even when the road seems difficult.
May you find in the smallest things
the courage to face any adversity,
and may you never be complicit
in injustice through silence.
May your voices always be
beacons of truth and hope.
Dad

Contents

Power and Privilage
    1. The Curse of the Montenegro Family   1
    2. The Privilege of Santiago   6
    3. Don Marcelo's Fall   11

Silence and Communication
    4. Laura's Silence   17
    5. The Pianist Silence   21
    6. Teresa's Silence   25
    7. Clara's Whispers   28

Resistance and Social Justice
    8. The Clamor of the Fields   35
    9. The Legend of Camila   40
    10. Gears of Freedom   45
    11. The Seeds of Sofía   50
    12. The Last Net   55

Tradition and Culture
    13. The Color of the Carnival   63
    14. The Mournings In The Coffee Plants   67
    15. The Weight of Bones   73

Dreams and Metaphors
    16. Juan's Last Dream   83
    17. Julián's Dream   87
    18. The Train of Dreams   91
    19. Faith In Uncertainty   94
    20. The Wind's Fragments   97

About the Author   103

Preface

This book brings together a collection of stories that have accompanied different stages of my life. Some were written in my youth, full of impulse and first ideas, and left forgotten, like something stored away to return to someday. Now, I've rescued, revised, and updated them to present them in a form more aligned with the present while striving to preserve that restless spirit that characterizes them.

Over the years, the ways of facing challenges have changed, but the tools remain the same: words, stories, and the small battles of daily life. These are my everyday weapons.

For the translation, I've worked to maintain the essence of each story in both languages. I didn't always adhere rigidly to the original text; sometimes, I prioritized rhythm and, other times, tone or structure, depending on what best conveyed the story.

I hope you enjoy these stories as much as I enjoyed writing them and giving them new life.

Power and Privilege

Chapter One

The Curse of the Montenegro Family

The entrance hall of former Congressman Carlos Montenegro's house was a furnace that noon. The thick air clung to the skin like a second layer of clothing while the distant murmur of the market seeped through the adobe walls. Two middle-aged men were engaged in a whispered conversation as if they feared their words would melt away in the heat. Ramiro, wearing his National Police Commander uniform, maintained a rigid posture that contradicted the beads of sweat sliding down his neck. Opposite him, Andrés dressed with studied simplicity, exuding the confidence that only knowing the right connections can keep you out of jail. His reputation as a thief was an open secret that his connections in the Senate had kept in the realm of rumors.

"It's been a while," Ramiro murmured, breaking the sticky silence of the afternoon.

"Same to you," Andrés replied with a smile barely touching his lips. "What have you been up to?"

"The usual. Running the Lucero Penitentiary, ensuring our 'guests' enjoy five-star accommodations," sarcasm dripped from every word Ramiro spoke. "And you?"

"The usual family business. Tough times call for creative measures," Andrés gestured dismissively with his hand as if swatting away an invisible fly.

"I can imagine how complicated that must be," Ramiro raised an eyebrow. "Especially with so much insecurity on the streets."

"Don't even get me started," Andrés replied. "These days, you can't even trust your own shadow."

The heavy air in the entrance hall carried words laden with double meanings. In the bedroom, Carlos Montenegro rested in his favorite armchair, his casted ankle elevated on a cushion. With eager eyes and boundless curiosity, his seven-year-old son, Alberto, watched him as one would observe a battle-wounded hero.

"Alberto, I'm going to tell you how I got hurt," Carlos began, settling into the armchair. "The game was tied, and we had to win. You know that we Montenegro are warriors; defeat isn't in our vocabulary."

The boy nodded, mesmerized as his father wove the story: Orlando's masterful pass, the rivals falling like dominoes, and that final cross that would have made Zidane himself pale.

"But," Carlos twisted his expression, "the defender mistook my leg for the ball. And here I am, two months out of the game."

The narration was interrupted by a voice that seemed to float above the heat. Aurora, the soul of the house, was in her impeccable uniform and with a serenity that seemed like a refuge against the midday swelter. Decades of service had made her more than just an employee; she was the silent guardian of family secrets, a second mother to Alberto.

"Excuse me, sir."

"Come in, Aurora."

"Ramiro and Andrés are waiting in the living room."

"Tell them to hold on a moment. I need a favor from them."

"As you wish, sir."

Aurora closed the door with the gentleness of someone who understood the weight of every silence. Alberto looked at his father with eyes full of miniature doctor's concern.

"Does it hurt a lot?"

"The day of the fracture was hell," Carlos admitted. "Now it's more bearable. The worst part will be the rehabilitation."

"But you're a warrior, right?"

"Until the end, champ."

Carlos tousled his son's hair, drawing a laugh that brightened the room. Aurora reappeared, her figure outlined against the doorframe.

"Sir, your monthly pension has arrived."

"Leave it on the table."

"Your wife called. She says it's urgent and needs me to send it."

"Don't worry, Aurora. I'll handle it."

The look Aurora gave Alberto was a poem of sweetness and concern, and the boy responded with a smile that held all the world's innocence. There was something in that silent exchange, a truth Alberto sensed without understanding. Carlos took the money and handed it to his son when they were alone.

"Champ, I need you to help me."

"Whatever you say, Dad."

"Take this money to the gentleman in the living room."

"Which one of the two?" Alberto asked, confused.

Carlos exhaled deeply as if preparing to release a bitter truth.

"Either one," he said with a crooked smile. "Either way, they're going to steal it from me."

Alberto took the money and left the room with the determination of a messenger who didn't understand the message he was carrying. Carlos stood by the window, lost in thoughts that weighed more than the heat of that afternoon, as a bitter smile drew the map of a defeat long foreseen across his face.

Chapter Two

The Privilege of Santiago

The career change of Roberto Arévalo, from civil engineering to law, had been one of those decisions that altered the course of entire generations. Not only had it led him to meet the woman who would become his wife, but it had also paved the way to his current position as mayor of the city. His rise had been methodical: first as a respected lawyer, then as secretary of the National

Socialist Party, and finally, the coveted municipal chair. This trajectory was not just a family story but a life manual for his son Santiago.

From as far back as he could remember, Santiago had watched, both fascinated and fearful, as his father wove an intricate web of favors and loyalties. Every handshake, every pat on the back, every calculated smile was a silent lesson that the young man absorbed: success was not a matter of merit but of surname and opportunity. By age twenty, Santiago had learned that his name not only opened doors but altered gravity, making heads bow as he passed.

The night had become his particular kingdom. While his friends wandered the alleys of pleasure with the clumsiness of beginners, negotiating prices with prostitutes amidst nervous laughter and crumpled bills, Santiago simply uttered the magic words: "I'm the mayor's son." It was like witnessing a tide change: the looks transformed, prices plummeted, and the best "professionals" vied for his attention. Privilege, he discovered, was a currency that never lost its value.

There wasn't a den of iniquity Santiago hadn't conquered. He moved through brothels, cantinas, and escort houses like a prince in his nocturnal court, always maintaining that air of superiority that borrowed money and a borrowed surname conferred upon him. However, to keep up appearances, he attended his classes at the Institute of Economic Careers with British punctuality. His journey through the business administration program felt like a lengthy bureaucratic procedure. It culminated in a barely decent grade point average. Still, his graduation became a political event where the rector, the governor, and even the president of Congress —who had traveled expressly from the capital— shook his hand amidst protocol smiles.

The post-graduation celebrations stretched on like a prolonged hangover until the time came for his first job interview. His parents anticipated this moment as the natural continuation of a dynasty of successes. However, the night before, Santiago had honored his monthly routine with his occasional "friends." The psychological tests were an open window to his obsessions: his fixation with prostitutes and his chaotic life were exposed like stains on an X-ray.

The technical tests only confirmed the obvious: Santiago shone more under neon lights than in front of an Excel screen. During the personal interview, when words tangled on his tongue like drunken snakes, he resorted to his usual spell: "I'm the mayor's son."

The waiting room turned into a suffocating purgatory where the candidates silently awaited the verdict. After two hours that felt like an eternity, the human resources director, a man who wore seriousness like armor, entered and pronounced with a judge's voice: —The selected candidate is Santiago Arévalo.

Santiago emerged from his stupor upon hearing his

name. He stood up with the slowness of someone waking from a nightmare while the gazes of the other candidates pierced him like poisoned darts. In his mind, a revelation crystallized with the force of a hangover: —«Damn, prestige doesn't work just with whores.».

Silas Dakar

Chapter Three

Don Marcelo's Fall

Don Marcelo was the perfect prototype of the local magnate: a man who had turned power into his religion and fear into his gospel. The extensive coffee plantations he owned stretched like a green sea as far as the eye could see, and his dominance over the people was so absolute that even the wind seemed to ask permission before blowing through his crops.

The walls of his estate told stories of power and

subjugation through carefully arranged family portraits and hunting trophies that stared blankly at visitors. Every object in that house was a reminder of his authority; every space breathed the arrogance of someone who has never known the word "no."

In that realm of silence and submission, Emiliano appeared like a crack in a wall everyone believed to be impregnable. He carried no more weapons than a worn notebook and a pen that dripped uncomfortable truths. His verses, born from sleepless nights and contained rage, were small revolutions gestating on paper.

At first, his poems were whispers in the corners, secrets shared between clenched teeth as workers returned from the coffee fields. But words have a life of their own, and soon, those verses began to fly through the market, slip between vegetable stalls, and resonate in plazas where even dogs seemed to pause and listen.

"The coffee plantations weep blood," Emiliano wrote, "and the black gold Don Marcelo sells drips the sweat of mothers who no longer have tears." His words painted pictures of children born with hunched backs, inheriting debts that not even their grandchildren could repay, and laborers who aged prematurely under a sun that knew no mercy.

The news of these poems reached Don Marcelo like a slap across the face. He summoned his close associates to the grand dining room of the estate, where crystal chandeliers watched the scene like silent witnesses to history.

"Who does that brat think he is?" he bellowed, his fist causing the mahogany table to tremble. "What does he know about building something? About sacrifice?"

The foremen exchanged uneasy glances. One of them, the oldest, dared to speak up: "With all due respect, boss, his words are sinking in deep. People are repeating them, memorizing them..."

"Let them whisper!" Don Marcelo interrupted. "Next time, I'll make sure those whispers are choked in their own throats."

That very night, as if the landlord's words had summoned him, Emiliano appeared in the main hall. He was dressed entirely in white like a ghost come to claim justice, and in his hands, he held a paper that seemed to glow with its own light.

With a clear and steady voice, without trembling, he read his final poem: "Don Marcelo, your coffee tastes of sweat and blood, each bean a tear you couldn't dry, every cup you sell is a future you kill, and your wealth is the hunger others cannot satiate."

The magnate, his face contorted with rage, ordered him to be expelled. But it was too late: the seed of rebellion had been planted, and like the best coffee, it had begun to ferment in the darkness.

That night, the coffee plantations witnessed whispered meetings, plans woven in the shadows of the trees that had watched over so much time. And at dawn, on the pristine white wall of the estate, a single word shone like a verdict: "JUSTICE."

Don Marcelo never reconciled to sleep in peace again. Emiliano's words, planted like rebellious seeds in the night, germinated beneath the fertile soil of injustice, growing with every whisper that swept through the town. Now, in the early mornings, it wasn't the roosters that woke him, but the verses seeping through the cracks of his estate, reminding him that some truths, like the best coffee, eventually awaken even the sleepiest, and revolutions, like poetry, refuse to die in silence.

Silence and Communication

Silas Dakar

Chapter Four

Laura's Silence

Laura Álvarez embodied a sublime contradiction: she possessed the timeless beauty of an Egyptian princess with the vibrant warmth of the Colombian Caribbean. It wasn't just her physical appearance that captivated; there was a serene elegance about her, a gaze that seemed to pierce through social masks to read the most intimate secrets of those around her. Her honey-colored eyes, exotic and deep, contrasted with the cascade of raven-black hair framing her face, while her long, shapely legs completed a presence that bordered on the mythological.

The vice president's farewell cocktail had turned into an absurd theater. Laura, exhausted from dodging prefabricated compliments and calculated smiles from attention-hungry executives, resorted to the last socially acceptable refuge: a trip to the restroom.

Her return to the lounge was like witnessing a goddess descending among mortals. Every step she took, marked by the innate rhythm of her native Cartagena, unleashed a wave of glances that she had learned to categorize with scientific precision: admiration, desire, envy, and that peculiar mix of all the above that only unattainable beauties generate. Laura navigated this sea of attention like someone who has learned to breathe underwater: with natural indifference.

In the most discreet corner of the lounge, like a discordant note in a perfectly orchestrated symphony, stood Luis. He was the quintessence of the ordinary and, therefore, invisible to most. Tall and slender as a reed, with glasses that seemed to amplify his perpetual observer aura, he watched the scene with the curiosity of an anthropologist accidentally invited to a tribal ritual. To him, these gatherings were an involuntary field study on human vanity: executives in designer suits exchanging inflated anecdotes and precisely measured laughs, all sprinkled with wine that likely exceeded his monthly food budget.

Emerging from his temporary refuge, Laura scanned the lounge with the precision of a radar. Among the pack of suited wolves devouring her with their gaze, her eyes settled on that solitary figure who seemed to exist in a parallel dimension to the party. With the grace of a feline, she glided toward him.

"Hi, I'm Laura. And you?" her voice was as soft as velvet.

"You look like a sphinx!" Luis's response sprang from his lips before his brain could censor it.

The blush that tinted Luis's cheeks contrasted with the naked truth Laura perceived in his eyes. A genuine smile spread across her face.

"Sorry, that was a reflex. I'm Luis," he hurried to correct.

"I'm Laura. What area do you work in?"

"Can't you guess?" he replied, aware that his scientist appearance was as obvious as a neon sign.

Finding unexpected pleasure in this game of feigned naivety, she decided to go with the flow.

"Human Resources?"

"No, but you're close. Research and Development. And you?"

"Marketing, I'm the director."

"You must be excellent to hold that position at such a young age."

"I graduated very young and have a lot of experience."

As they conversed, their world blurred like a painting under the rain. The pack of executives watched with a mix of disbelief and annoyance as their most coveted prey willingly surrendered to the claws of the most unlikely hunter. Whispers slithered among the glasses: "How is this possible?" "He must have something we don't see." Some tried to maintain a façade of indifference, though their eyes betrayed an almost painful curiosity about this strange twist in the social script.

Aware of the chaos she had unleashed, Laura seemed to enjoy the moment with an almost mischievous pleasure. Luis's authenticity had captivated her just as her beauty had captivated others for years. For his part, he experienced the strange sensation of having won a prize for which he hadn't even bought a ticket.

At the end of the evening, when empty glasses clinked like victory bells, Laura took Luis's hand with a decision that even surprised herself. She led him out of the lounge into a night that promised to reveal that sometimes, very few times, silence speaks louder than a thousand words, and that true passion doesn't always roar like a wolf but whispers like a long-guarded secret.

Chapter Five

The Pianist Silence

The Bar Tayrona, with its chipped walls and fans spinning like lazy propellers, was the last bastion of old music in Getsemaní. Every night, Daniel sat in front of the black grand piano, an inheritance from more glamorous times, and let his fingers glide over the keys, searching for something lost in the ether. From the balcony of the colonial house across the street, among bougainvilleas spilling over like a cascade of purple, Elena watched him with the same fascination as someone reading a secret score. Her silhouette, outlined against the yellow light of her room, had become an indispensable part of the neighborhood's nighttime landscape.

"I swear it's the most beautiful romance I've ever seen," said Doña Carmen, the woman from the corner café with arepas, leaning on the doorframe. "He plays only for her."

"And she only appears on her balcony when she hears the first notes of the piano," added Joaquín, the old waiter who served rum with the same elegance as if directing an imaginary orchestra. "You can see their faces look like lovers from my table."

The neighbors sighed as they witnessed the scene that repeated every night: Daniel, impeccable in his white guayabera and silver temples, playing while looking toward the balcony; Elena, in her floral dresses, drinking in every movement of his hands over the keys. No one in the neighborhood suspected that Daniel had never heard his own melodies. Meningitis had left him deaf as a child, and his mother—a pianist as well—taught him to feel the music at his fingertips, in the vibration of each key.

Elena, from her balcony, also couldn't hear a single note. An accident had plunged her into a world of silence, but she had learned to "listen" to the music in Daniel's hands, in the sway of his body, and in the way the dim lights of the bar reflected on her sweat-beaded forehead. Every night, as she watched him play, she would squint her eyes, convinced that this was how she deciphered each measure he created.

"Don't they ever talk?" asked a stranger, surprised to see such a silent connection. "Who knows if they need to talk," Doña Carmen replied, shrugging her shoulders. "Honestly, I'm happy just watching them."

One October night, so hot that the breeze felt like an exhausted whisper, Elena descended the stairs of her house, crossed the cobblestone street, and entered the bar just as Daniel was playing a melody that sounded like a bolero, or a love ballad, or maybe both. Immediately, the customers fell silent. Not even the rum dared to clink in the glasses. Daniel looked up from the piano and met her eyes for the first time, without a balcony between them. Then, she moved her hands in the air, drawing signs that he understood instantly. Without thinking, Daniel responded with the same delicacy, abandoning the keys to speak to her in that silent language they both shared.

"What are they doing?" murmured a girl behind the bar, intrigued. "They're telling each other everything," Joaquín replied, smiling so that his face wrinkled. "It's sign language... Both of them are deaf."

At that moment, Daniel stood up, took Elena's hands, and, in that silence where only they could hear the purest music, they began to dance. The piano fell silent, and yet, something still resonated in the air, something that beat in the way their bodies moved in unison. Doña Carmen, unintentionally, let out a tender sob. The old women of the neighborhood wiped away tears of emotion. It was clear that, for Daniel and Elena, the music had never been in the sounds: they felt it in the touch of their fingers, in the warmth of their gazes, in the rhythm they marked together without needing to hear a single chord.

Chapter Six

Teresa's Silence

Teresa had watched more promises pass by than seasons from her window. Her house, on a corner of the main square, was the perfect vantage point to observe how power changed faces but not vices. Her wrinkles were a map of disillusionment, and her eyes were deep wells where lies sank.

The town's inhabitants respected her, not for what she said, but for what she kept silent. Teresa hoarded people's secrets like ancient coins, knowing precisely when and how to use them. From her rocking chair, she witnessed the endless dance of those in power: candidates who arrived with dazzling smiles and left behind broken promises; officials who swore change but, in reality, delivered the same continuity.

The favored candidate's visit was inevitable. He arrived on a stifling afternoon when the heat melted lies at lightning speed. His entourage resembled a traveling circus: advisors in flashy suits, restless photographers, sycophants with mechanical applause. Teresa welcomed them with the composure of someone who had seen too many come and go.

The candidate, self-assured, sat before her with the arrogance of someone who couldn't fathom rejection. Teresa poured tea into cups so old they had heard more promises than any ballot box.

"Mrs. Teresa," he began with his brightest smile, "this time, everything will be different, I assure you."

"Different?" Teresa poured the tea unhurriedly. "Like when your father came to promise me the same? Or your grandfather?"

The candidate shifted uncomfortably in his seat.

"Times have changed. We have projects, plans…"

"Do you know what happens to empty promises?" Teresa interrupted. "The wind takes them away, but the scars remain."

He swallowed hard.

"I assure you my intentions…"

"The people don't forget, son," she gently cut him off. "Promises, like the wind, come and go, but they never quench the thirst."

"With all due respect, ma'am, you don't understand modern politics."

Teresa smiled with the wisdom of many decades.

"No, son. It's you who don't understand that power is borrowed while the memory of the people is eternal."

Her words fell like stones into a pond. The candidate, so accustomed to controlling every conversation, was left without a script. His entourage, once noisy, fell into absolute silence. Teresa continued pouring tea as if she were only discussing the weather.

The visit ended without much ceremony. The candidate and his entourage departed, leaving behind a trail of promises and wounded pride. From her window, Teresa watched as the wind carried away dry leaves and lies alike.

"The winds change, but the roots remain," she murmured as the afternoon settled over the town like an old blanket.

From that day forward, power learned to steer clear of Teresa's house. Her silence became a monument more revered than any statue in the square, for everyone knew that within that silence lay a truth no political speech could alter: that power is fleeting, but the memory of the people is eternal.

Chapter Seven

Clara's Whispers

The municipal library was Clara's silent kingdom, a labyrinth of shelves where forbidden truths were hidden in plain sight. Her steps, light and precise, navigated the aisles with the familiarity of someone who knows every corner.

"The best books aren't on the shelves," she whispered one afternoon to Pedro, a twelve-year-old boy searching for something more than simple stories in the letters.

Inspector González, seated at his desk near the entrance, looked up warily. The disarray of papers before him seemed like an excuse to keep an eye on every movement.

"What are you talking about?" he inquired, raising an eyebrow.

"I recommend the approved fables, Inspector," Clara said with a smile. "As always."

Pedro averted his gaze, but his mind kept turning over her words. There was something in Clara's tone, a spark that ignited questions impossible to extinguish. As evening fell, when the sun timidly filtered through the tall windows and the inspector nodded off from fatigue, Clara guided the boy toward the basement.

"My husband and I started hiding them when the burnings began," she whispered as they descended the creaky stairs, each step groaning in protest.

"What burnings?" Pedro asked, trying to adjust his eyes to the dimness that enveloped the space.

"The burnings of books, ideas, dreams," Clara explained, moving a bookshelf to reveal a secret room. "Every volume here is a survivor."

Dust swirled in the beams of light filtering through a narrow crack, lending the space an almost sacred atmosphere. The room was filled with banned works: poetry that exalted freedom, stories with uncomfortable truths, philosophy that taught critical thinking.

"Why are you showing this to me?" Pedro whispered, reverently stroking the dusty spines.

"Because I see in your eyes the same hunger for truth I saw in my Antonio's," Clara replied, removing her glasses, her gaze weighted with memories. "Before they took him away."

The silence filled the room, but it was not oppressive; it was an unspoken pact between generations. From then on, Pedro visited the library frequently, and soon other children also arrived, chosen with great caution. Clara taught them to read between the lines, to question, and to commit forbidden truths to memory as if they were small treasures.

One day, Inspector González approached with a stern expression.

"The children are asking strange questions at school, Clara."

"Children always ask questions, Inspector. It's in their nature."

"Nature can be dangerous, just like the wrong books," he warned, leaning over his desk.

"As dangerous as the fear of questions," she responded softly but firmly.

That very night, Clara and the children moved the books to a new hiding place. Each box they carried was a testament to resistance. A week later, when the inspectors raided the basement, they found only dust and empty shelves. The forbidden words, meanwhile, continued to spread quietly through the classrooms and corners of the village, germinating in the minds of a generation hungry for freedom.

Years later, when the regime finally fell, no one connected the revolution to the elderly librarian who continued cataloging books with meticulous precision. Only the children, now adults, knew that that force—born from a whisper in the basement—had torn down walls that weapons could not breach.

Silas Dakar

Resistance
and
Social Justice

Silas Dakar

Chapter Eight

The Clamor of the Fields

The earth clung to Rubén's hands like a second skin—black, fertile, a silent witness to generations of toil. The furrow he plowed ran deep, like the scars of injustice that had carved their mark on these ancestral fields.

"Your father knew how to work this land," said the overseer from the window of his gleaming new truck, the polished metal a sharp contrast to the dust-covered road.

"He knew how to respect hierarchies."

Rubén kept digging, each strike of his hoe a silent act of defiance, each cut into the soil a verse of rebellion.

"Times are changing, boss," he said without looking up.

"The land doesn't change, Rubén," the overseer replied, lighting an imported cigarette, his breath exhaling superiority along with the smoke. "Neither do the ones who own it."

In the neighboring furrow, Mariela tightened her grip on the wooden handle of her tool until her knuckles turned as white as bone beneath the skin. Her son, Juan, played nearby, building castles with the very soil that refused to belong to them—his tiny hands molding the future without knowing it. Mariela looked toward the horizon, where the shadows of the hills seemed to guard a secret only the farmers could understand. The chirping of crickets filled the air, blending with the crunch of earth beneath their tools like an ancient song of struggle.

That night, in the communal house lit by flickering kerosene lamps, the farmers gathered. The air smelled of freshly brewed coffee and accumulated exhaustion—hope and fear intertwined.

"How much longer, Rubén?" asked Don Jacinto, his trembling hands gripping a chipped cup as though holding on to his last bit of hope. "I lost my son in these fields. How much longer will we keep planting dreams in borrowed soil?"

Rubén looked around at the sun-scarred faces, at the eyes

darkened by years of waiting. Every wrinkle told a story, every scar was a line in an unwritten history of sacrifice.

"The land has memory," he said. "It remembers who truly works it."

"What you're proposing is dangerous," interjected a young man, his hands marked by old battles. "You saw what happened at the neighboring hacienda."

"It's more dangerous for our children to inherit our chains," Mariela's voice rose from the back of the room, Juan asleep in her arms like a seed of the future. Her words echoed in the thick silence. The farmers exchanged glances—determination and fear flickering in their eyes, like lightning before a storm.

Resistance, like plants, begins from below, taking root in silence. First, it was small acts—seeds hidden away, tools mysteriously disappearing, harvests yielding inexplicably less. The tension grew, whispering through the wind and the earth. The old wooden floors of the communal house bore witness to clandestine meetings and murmured conspiracies, multiplying like leaves carried by the wind.

The foreman noticed the changes first, like an animal sensing a storm in the air.

"Something's happening, boss. The land isn't yielding the same."

"It's them," the overseer muttered, his cigarette trembling with rage, an unfulfilled threat hanging in the smoke. "They're planning something."

Before dawn, before the sun kissed the hills, the farmers took the fields. There were no shouts, no violence—only the silent, unwavering presence of hundreds of men and women standing in the land they had watered with their sweat for generations, rooted like ancient trees. Dew glistened on the leaves, as if the earth itself was weeping with relief.

The overseer arrived with the police, but he found a wall of silence stronger than any fence. The farmers simply kept working, indifferent to threats and eviction orders, as one ignores the passing wind.

"This land has memory," Rubén said when the overseer demanded to speak with him. "And it remembers who has truly worked it."

The negotiations lasted for weeks. When the shared ownership agreement was finally signed, Mariela found Rubén standing in the same old field, where it had all begun. The afternoon sun bathed the furrows in golden light, as if the land itself were celebrating.

"Was the risk worth it?" she asked, her voice trembling between exhaustion and hope.

Rubén took a handful of earth and let it slip through his fingers, like grains in a natural hourglass. In the distance, Juan played among the furrows, his small hands buried in the same soil his parents had fought for.

"The land always knew it belonged to us," he said,

watching his son with a quiet smile. "But today, for the first time, we know it too."

Chapter Nine

The Legend of Camila

In the heart of the neighborhood, where the streets still held the flavor of old stories, Camila kneaded dreams every dawn. Her hands, weathered by years of work and hope, knew the secret language of flour and yeast. She wasn't just a baker; she was the guardian of a tradition that fed something more than just stomachs.

Her bakery, a humble yet immaculate storefront, was

the first place to awaken each day. Long before the sun dared to peek, the aroma of freshly baked bread already snaked through the streets like a warm embrace, with sweet notes that caressed the soul and the promise of a crispy crust in every bite. People said her bread had a secret ingredient impossible to copy, though Camila would only smile when it was mentioned. Perhaps it was her habit of listening to each customer's stories, storing their sorrows and joys like one preserves sourdough, with care and devotion.

The entire neighborhood measured itself by her oven's schedule: workers knew it was time to leave when the first loaf came out, children ran to school with pockets full of sweet bread, and afternoons closed with the scent of the last batch. Camila didn't just sell bread; she gave dignity in every boule, hope in every roll.

When the new mayor, drunk on power and hungry for control, decided to impose an exorbitant tax on bakers, he never imagined he would find his greatest resistance in a woman barely reaching five feet tall. The news hit the neighborhood like an unexpected storm, and Camila, with a determination that surprised even those who had known her all their lives, called all the bakers to her shop.

"What are we going to do, Camila?" asked Don Pedro, the oldest of them all, while wiping his eternally white flour-covered hands on his worn apron.

Don Pedro, with his calloused hands and the worn apron

he had worn since his youth, let out a sigh that carried both resignation and love for his craft.

Camila, with a voice that seemed to draw strength from generations of bakers before her, responded, "If they take our bread today, tomorrow they'll take the air we breathe. We can't allow it!"

While the other bakers resignedly accepted the new tax, bending their backs under the weight of a new injustice, Camila stood firm like the best of her loaves. She organized a silent strike, a protest measured not in shouts but in absences.

The city woke the next day to a silence that hurt. There was no scent of freshly baked bread, no warmth emanating from the bakeries, no daily ritual that marked the pulse of life itself. The shutters of each bakery were like closed eyelids refusing to see more injustice. The silence weighed heavily, like a storm waiting to break.

Discontent grew like the best dough. People began to understand that bread was not just food; it was a symbol of something deeper: the dignity of honest work, the right to earn a living with hands and sweat. Like dough that needs time to rise, the neighborhood's resistance grew slowly, gaining strength with each day of the strike.

When the mayor was finally forced to withdraw the tax, defeated by the will of a woman who had turned bread into a symbol of resistance, Camila returned to her oven. That morning, she placed a sign in her window that simply read:

"Today, Bread is Free."

Tears rolled down the customers' faces, mixing with the crumbs of bread in their hands. In every smile, in every gaze, one truth was clear: they had reclaimed more than their bread; they had reclaimed their dignity.

And thus her legend was born. That day, Camila's bread tasted sweeter than ever because it was made of freedom and shared will. Those who tasted it understood that dignity, like fermented dough, needs time and courage to grow; and that sometimes, the greatest strength rises from a humble oven on any street. Since then, every boule that left her hands carried a steadfast message: a neighborhood fed with hope will never let itself be kneaded by injustice again.

Silas Dakar

Chapter Ten

Gears of Freedom

Time had a sanctuary in the village, and that was Don Esteban's workshop. The walls were lined with antique clocks—some pendulums swaying like silent sentinels, others with hands worn down by decades of telling stories—all ticking in perfect harmony, breathing life into the space. There, the old watchmaker had built his empire of gears and seconds, a refuge where his hands, as precise as the mechanisms he repaired, turned each broken piece into a melody of time itself.

Every morning, the villagers synchronized their watches with the chimes from his shop: a tradition as old as the village square itself, a ritual that, unbeknownst to them, synchronized more than just time.

"Clocks are like people, Ricardo," Don Esteban would say to his young apprentice, adjusting a delicate mechanism on the workbench with the precision of someone who manipulates fate itself. "Some run ahead, others lag behind, but all can be tuned—if you touch the right pieces and have the patience to do so."

Ricardo, his eyes always curious like hands searching for the exact hour, saw his master as an alchemist, transforming seconds into hope, weaving the invisible gears of the town's destiny. He listened with devotion, mesmerized by how those wrinkled hands, guided by tiny screwdrivers and expert magnifying glasses, turned chaos into order, slowness into punctuality, as if arranging the universe one cog at a time.

At dusk, the bell above the door rang, clear as a note of freedom. Carmen, the florist from the plaza, stepped inside carrying a small package wrapped in newspaper, concealing more than just seeds.

"Don Esteban, the seeds you requested have arrived," she announced, placing them on the counter with the practiced ease of someone who had rehearsed the gesture a thousand times.

"The yellow roses?" the watchmaker inquired, never lifting his gaze from the open clock on the table, a promise in the making.

"Yes, and also the red carnations," she replied, her hands stained with earth, her voice blooming with quiet strength as she cast a knowing glance toward the back room, where something more than flowers was taking root.

Ricardo, meticulously polishing the shop's glass display until it gleamed like the future they dreamed of, couldn't quite grasp his master's sudden interest in gardening.

When night fell, Don Esteban's workshop transformed into a stage of intrigue and revolution. The soft glow of oil lamps illuminated disassembled clocks—skeletal remains of a freedom yet to come—while the rhythmic ticking merged with hushed voices tracing the blueprint of an inevitable change. Behind an old curtain, the back room became the beating mechanical heart of the uprising. Álvaro, an engineering student whose eyes burned like the spark of hope, gathered there with other young men. They all surrounded the old man, who unveiled the magic of clocks turned into something far greater than mere timekeepers.

"Each clock is a key," Don Esteban whispered, pointing to the modified mechanisms with the precision of a surgeon of time. "And each key will open a door to freedom."

"Do you think they'll suspect us?" Manuel, the most

cautious of the group, asked one night when silence wrapped the village like a blanket of complicity.

"Who would ever suspect an old watchmaker?" Don Esteban replied, offering a near-paternal smile that concealed the ticking of revolution. "To them, I am merely the guardian of time."

The clandestine network grew like a vine of precise seconds and minutes. The modified clocks left the workshop in elegant gift boxes, and though at first glance they seemed like ordinary timepieces, their hands marked more than just hours—they counted the heartbeats of an impending revolution.

"Master, why so many new pieces?" Ricardo dared to ask, watching the growing stacks of clocks like soldiers awaiting orders.

"Because there are moments when time needs a push," the old man said, his gaze fixed on a particularly intricate gear that held the secret of freedom. "And we are here to give it."

The appointed day arrived with the precision of a Swiss chronometer. At midnight, as the village slept beneath a sky full of complicit stars, Don Esteban's clocks awoke in perfect synchronization, a mechanical army springing to life. A symphony of ticking grew louder, vibrating through the air like the prelude to a long-awaited storm—until it gave way to the deafening roar of explosions. Sparks and flashes tore through the night like fireworks of liberation, as the echoes of each detonation spread across the valley like a cry of victory. From every corner of the village, columns of smoke rose like clocks striking the dawn of a new era, each explosion marking the rhythm of a revolution that had been silently forged between hands and gears.

Time, which had always been his silent ally, was now keeping pace with a new kind of freedom.

Don Esteban smiled. He had spent his entire life studying time, perfecting it, tuning it—and now, finally, time worked for him. As the first rays of sunlight kissed the plaza, he watched his work unfold and knew, with certainty, that every revolution, like the finest timepieces, required precision, patience, and the courage of those willing to wind the clock of destiny.

Chapter Eleven

The Seeds of Sofía

Sofía's house, perched atop the hill like an open book beneath the sky, was far more than a simple dwelling—it stood as a beacon, casting flickers of stories and hope across the valley. Its windows, forever open like windblown pages, let fragments of tales escape, carried by the breeze to the darkest corners of the village, like seeds of freedom searching for fertile ground.

Every afternoon, a chorus of children's footsteps climbed the steep street, eager to settle in the old woman's small patio, where her words wove worlds that no censorship could ever contain—threads of light piercing the darkness.

María, a girl with rebellious braids that danced like question marks and a gaze sharpened by truth, always arrived before the others. She had lost her parents in the protests the previous year, and in Sofía's stories, she found clues and answers no one else dared to mention—buried treasures hidden in parables.

"Tell us again the one about the king who was afraid," the children would ask, their eyes glowing like tiny torches of curiosity.

Sofía, whose gaze carried the memory of three generations like the pages of an ancestral book, would smile and begin with her usual phrase, each word laden with meaning: "Once upon a time, there was a kingdom where silence was law. But remember, children, silence has echoes, and echoes have memory."

The adults passing by pretended not to hear those tales, yet their steps grew slower, their ears more attentive—like dry leaves halted by the wind of truth. Sofía's stories were like stones cast into a pond; the ripples spread far beyond what anyone could foresee, reaching distant shores of awareness.

"Why was the king so afraid?" little Lucas dared to ask one day, his voice as clear as spring water.

"Because stories are seeds," Sofía replied, casting a knowing glance toward the parents pausing on the sidewalk, drawn in like birds to scattered crumbs. "And seeds, sooner or later, bloom into gardens of freedom."

One afternoon, Tomás, the baker, finally gathered the courage to approach, just after closing his shop. His apron, still dusted white with flour, fluttered like a flag of surrender before the truth.

"Your stories remind me of other times, Mrs. Sofía," he said, his voice laced with nostalgia, the kind that smells of freshly baked bread.

"Stories are like bread, Tomás," she replied, her voice imbued with the warmth of ancestral wisdom, flowing like honey through the cracks of fear. "They nourish the spirit and feed hope."

Little by little, those tales took on a life of their own—like seeds sprouting in fertile soil. The children repeated them at home, the adults whispered them after dinner like prayers for freedom, and the neighbors passed them from mouth to mouth along the cobblestone streets, where every stone bore silent witness to the quiet revolution growing in words.

One evening, the military surrounded the plaza, their boots hammering fear into the cobblestones, each step a heavy punctuation mark of oppression. Terror threatened to descend like an unannounced storm.

Yet Sofía, seated in her patio like a queen in her garden

of stories, continued her tale of a village that had lost its fear.

In response, the neighbors stepped onto their balconies—not to shout, not to fight, but to tell stories.

Hundreds of voices, rising as one, narrating the tales Sofía had planted. Each word bloomed like a flower breaking through the cracks of silence.

María, now taller, her braids longer like vines of rebellion, squeezed the old woman's hand.

"See, Mrs. Sofía?" she whispered, certainty shining in her eyes. "Your stories are stronger than their weapons."

Sofía smiled, for she knew that revolutions, like the greatest stories, always begin with "Once upon a time" and end with a people who find their voice—one that grows beyond the reach of any shadow, blooming into the inevitable spring of freedom.

Silas Dakar

Chapter Twelve

The Last Net

A t four in the morning, while the Caribbean stars still flickered over La Boquilla, the humble coastal village where generations of fishermen had passed down their craft like a sacred rite, old Ernesto was already on his boat. The tired engine coughed and sputtered against the waves, its familiar rhythm a lullaby to the sleeping village. His fishing net, worn thin by the years, danced in the water like a silver ghost chasing shadows. It was the same ancient ritual: the sea breathing beneath him, the sky watching from above, and the eternal hope of a good catch before the sun split the horizon.

Across the city, in a world far removed from fish scales and salt spray, Mayor Martínez was bidding farewell to foreign businessmen in the opulent lounge of Hotel Caribe—that bastion of luxury where the destinies of the coast were decided over crystal glasses filled with imported whiskey. Under the golden glow of chandeliers, they spread out their glossy blueprints on mahogany tables, their fingers pointing eagerly at a particular render.

"Look, Mr. Mayor," one of the men said, his foreign accent thick with enthusiasm. "This stretch of beach is perfect for the new dock."

"It's the project of the century," the mayor grinned, loosening his silk tie with practiced ease. "Marina Real will be the jewel of the Caribbean. Just imagine all the jobs it will create!"

By the time the sun had fully risen, Ernesto was guiding his boat back to shore. The morning's catch—small, meager—was barely worth the fuel spent. Beneath the shade of an old almond tree, he sat mending his net while an aging radio crackled beside him. Between bursts of static, it played vallenatos—those accordion-fueled laments of love, loss, and the eternal struggle between tradition and change.

"Progress for all!" the broadcaster's voice cut through the

music. "The mega-project will generate over a thousand jobs!"

"Progress?" Ernesto muttered, knotting his thread with the patience of a man who had lived through too many promises. "As if fish could swim in concrete."

His hands—gnarled, sturdy, like the roots of the mangroves that had once cradled his village—moved with the precision of half a century at sea. Every knot was a story. Every tear in the net, a memory of dawns spent chasing the tide.

Just then, his grandson, Toñito, came racing down the beach, his feet kicking up small clouds of sand, a crumpled newspaper clutched in his hands.

"Look, Grandpa! There's a picture of the hotel they're going to build!" the boy exclaimed, eyes bright with the promise of something new and gleaming.

Ernesto adjusted his wire-rimmed glasses, studying the photo of Mayor Martínez, golden scissors in hand, smiling as he cut the inaugural ribbon. He handed the paper back without a word and returned to his net.

"And have you decided about that bellhop training course, Toñito?" he asked quietly. "The vocational school is offering it for free."

"The teacher says they'll give us uniforms and everything," the boy answered, his voice buzzing with excitement for a future that drifted further from the sea with each passing day.

The afternoon was thick with heat when Marcos, the man from the tourist restaurant, arrived. His Hawaiian shirt clashed against the muted colors of the fishing village, and his polished shoes gleamed in the sun—shoes that had clearly never known the feel of a boat deck or the weight of a net.

"Don Ernesto, I have a proposal for you," he said, pulling a thick envelope from his pocket. "The investors want to buy all the fishing boats to turn them into bay tour cruises."

"Bay tours?" Ernesto looked up from his work. "And what about the fish?"

"Modern times, Mr. Ernesto. People prefer imported salmon now. Our local catch doesn't sell anymore." Marcos shrugged, dismissing centuries of tradition with the flick of his wrist.

In the distance, the first excavators growled, biting into the sacred stretch of sand where Ernesto's father had once taught him to read the tides. Where, for generations, men had cast their nets under the moon's careful watch.

It was the same patch of earth where, just hours earlier, the mayor had stood before the cameras, boasting of a "bright future for all."

That night, beneath a moon that sketched silver pathways across the dark waters, Ernesto and the other fishermen cast their nets for the last time.

They worked in silence, each motion heavy with the weight of something ending.

At dawn, when the executives and reporters arrived for the groundbreaking ceremony, the camera flashes illuminated a beach covered in dead fish and torn nets.

"What is the meaning of this?" the mayor demanded, covering his nose with a silk handkerchief, his polished shoes stepping carefully around the rotting catch.

From his stranded boat, Ernesto simply shrugged.

Still smiling that same quiet, bitter smile, he replied:

"The future, Mr. Mayor. The very one you're selling us."

Silas Dakar

Tradition and Culture

Silas Dakar

Chapter Thirteen

The Color of the Carnival

Rosa's house was alive with the scents of carnival—compact powders mingling with the sweet, sharp smell of sequin glue that adorned the costumes of the Comparsa del Congo Grande, one of the most respected African-influenced dance troupes in the carnival. Between walls painted in colors that had faded under countless summer suns, an old fan chopped uselessly at the thick air.

From the living room came the heartbeat of the carnival itself: the primal rhythm of drums accompanied by the haunting wail of the traditional bagpipe, as dancers rehearsed their steps for the grand parade.

On the front porch, Rosa was meticulously applying Miyoral's white base makeup. The queen of the comparsa sat perfectly still, her face a canvas half-completed, though even now she couldn't help but move slightly to the music with that natural grace that had made her the obvious choice to lead the troupe.

"Stay still, my queen," Rosa cautioned, holding her brush aloft like a conductor's baton. "If you sweat now, everything will run, and not even all the glitter in the world will save us."

Miyoral sighed, her eyes drifting toward the interior of the house where laughter and music seemed to push the temperature even higher. The drums pulsed in perfect synchronization with her anxious heart.

"I just want everything to be perfect," she whispered, her gaze fixed on something only she could see.

Inside, Daniel was keeping spirits high with a stream of jokes and generous pours of aguardiente, the potent local spirit that fueled countless carnival celebrations. Meanwhile, Pacho, the veteran drummer whose hands had kept time for more generations of dancers than anyone could remember, was practicing his rhythms with such infectious energy that the very floorboards seemed to dance beneath their feet.

"Hey, Rosa!" Daniel's voice boomed from the living room. "How's our Miyoral looking? Is she ready to steal the show or what?"

"Quiet, you! I'm working my magic here!" Rosa called back with a laugh. Then, lowering her voice to a gentle murmur, she added to Miyoral, "Almost finished, dear."

Miyoral, typically towering and radiant with joy, seemed unusually restless today. Her eyes darted between the street and her reflection, as if searching for answers in both.

"Any sign of Mono?" she asked, peering down the sun-baked street. Her brother's nickname, earned from his shock of blonde hair that glowed like a beacon in the Caribbean sun, had long since replaced his given name in everyone's hearts. "He promised to come help me practice the final step."

"Your brother will be here soon enough," Rosa assured her, adjusting a paper flower in Miyoral's elaborate hairstyle. "You know him—always the life of the party."

The world shattered with the sudden crack of gunfire—three sharp reports that silenced the drums as if they'd never played at all. Miyoral's hand flew to her chest, her heart stuttering beneath her fingers. For one eternal moment, the world hung suspended, with only the echoes of those shots bouncing between the buildings like trapped birds.

"What in God's name...?" Rosa's words barely escaped her lips.

Then came the cry that would haunt their dreams forever:

"Mono! They've killed Mono!"

Miyoral felt reality crumble around her. She sat frozen, the paper flower slowly slipping from her hair, as she felt her carefully applied makeup begin to run. A single tear carved through the white base—a thick, oily streak that left a pale path of devastation in its wake.

Daniel burst from the house, his face still bright with carnival joy that died the instant he saw Miyoral's expression.

"What's wrong?" he asked, confusion giving way to dread as his eyes followed the growing crowd in the street. "What...?"

Pacho had emerged too, but fell silent at the sight of Mono's motionless form on the sun-baked asphalt. The drum slipped from his fingers, its hollow thud a final beat in the terrible silence.

"Dear God..." The words escaped him like a prayer.

Rosa stood transfixed, the makeup brush still suspended in her hand, taking in the terrible tableau before her: the screams that tore through the afternoon heat, Miyoral's contained sobs, the violent absence of music. She swallowed hard and whispered with bitter wisdom:

"Damn... Makeup doesn't just mask faces; it conceals sorrows. And the carnival, even though it colors sadness, doesn't erase it completely."

Chapter Forteen

The Mournings In The Coffee Plants

No one dared set foot on El Paraíso farm after sunset. The coffee pickers ended their day the moment the sun threatened to vanish behind the dark green hills, and even the dogs sought shelter before the night draped the coffee fields in a cloak of shadows and secrets.

Don Jacinto, the farm's overseer, watched the daily exodus from the veranda of the big house, his calloused hands wrapped around a steaming cup of coffee.

"There's nothing to be done, kid," he said one evening to Alfonso, the new foreman, as the sky burned in streaks of violet and orange. "These people swear a ghost roams these fields. My grandfather used to tell me the same thing when I was a boy. They say that twenty years ago, in these very plantations, a foreman beat a girl so brutally that she lost her leg… and they still hear her screams when night falls."

Alfonso, accustomed to ghost stories from his own village across the mountain, shrugged, though he couldn't stop the chill that ran down his spine like an icy spider.

"You know how these things go, Don Jacinto," he replied, adjusting his sun-worn hat. "Sometimes people need a ghost to justify their fears."

Don Jacinto let out a snort, his breath carrying the scent of freshly brewed coffee.

"That's what I thought too. But I've seen it with my own eyes—on those nights, not even the dogs dare to bark."

The next morning, both men had breakfast in the wide kitchen, where the wood stove spread its ancestral warmth and old pewter pots hung from beams blackened by time.

"Listen, Alfonso," Don Jacinto said, watching the steam from his cup curl in the cold morning air, "don't let those ghost stories get in your head. Today we need to make sure not a single coffee bean goes missing from the harvest."

Alfonso nodded.

"Of course, sir. But is it true about the thefts at night?"

Don Jacinto took a slow sip of coffee, as bitter as his thoughts.

"Whole sacks have disappeared overnight. The boss thinks someone's using the 'Patasola' legend to scare the pickers and steal under cover of darkness."

"Then tonight, I'll stay until midnight and find out the truth."

"Are you sure, Alfonso? Even the last foremen wouldn't stay after dark."

Alfonso stood up and tightened the laces of his boots.

"My mother lost her leg three months ago. Diabetes. She's bedridden in a shack on the other side of the mountain. If there's one thing I've learned, it's that fear doesn't help anyone."

Don Jacinto sighed, clapping a hand on his shoulder.

"You're a brave one, kid. But still… be careful."

That night, under a full moon that turned the coffee fields into a silver ocean, Alfonso stayed behind.

Armed with a flashlight and a machete, he checked the sacks and locked up the tools. The wind slipped through the coffee plants like an ancient lament, the rustling leaves whispering secrets only the night could understand.

First, a murmur.

Then, a moan, stretching, bending, until it rose into a scream so raw it made his blood curdle.

"Who's there?" he forced himself to shout, though his

voice trembled.

The air thickened, pressing against his ribs like an invisible weight.

Through the tangled shadows, something moved.

A figure swayed between the rows of coffee plants with an unnatural, lurching gait.

Alfonso's flashlight trembled in his hands, the weak beam flickering over damp earth. The sharp scent of freshly cut coffee filled his nostrils, but beneath it was something else—something rotting, something buried.

Then she stepped into the moonlight.

Her dress, torn and caked in dried blood and red soil, clung to her frail frame.

Her face, both terrifying and eerily beautiful, bore the weight of eternal grief.

And where her left leg should have been, there was only a chasm of blackness—a void so deep it swallowed the light itself.

Alfonso's body refused to move.

Then, his breath caught—because in her eyes, he saw what she had seen.

Memories that were not his rushed through him in flashes:

The girl's hands plucking coffee beans.

Her voice, firm, accusing the foreman of stealing her wages.

The fists, the boots, the merciless beating.

Her screams, swallowed by the silent hills.

Her broken body, left to rot beneath the weight of the night.

Tears burned in Alfonso's eyes.

"My mother," he whispered, his voice cracking. "She's losing her other leg too. Because medicine never arrives."

The Patasola stopped.

Her rage flickered, if only for a moment.

For the first time, there was something else in her expression—a sliver of recognition, of understanding.

Slowly, she raised a skeletal hand, pointing toward the twisted roots of an ancient tree.

Alfonso, his heart hammering, stepped forward and dug into the damp earth.

There, beneath the roots, he unearthed a rusted metal box.

Inside were documents—proof of decades of stolen wages, exploitation, and cold indifference.

For an instant, he felt the chill of her touch on his hand. When he looked up—she was gone.

The next morning, Alfonso placed the papers before Don Jacinto.

The old man flipped through them in silence, his face pale.

Without hesitation, Alfonso rode into town. By noon, the provincial authorities had the evidence in their hands.

The stories of the Patasola's screams continued, but there were no new victims.

Instead, whispers spread of medicine arriving on time

to the remote villages.

Of Alfonso's mother, walking again with a new prosthetic and a quiet smile.

Of higher wages, better oversight, fewer stolen lives.

Alfonso never spoke of that night, but he would always remember the Patasola's anguished eyes.

She could have destroyed him.

But she didn't.

And in that moment, he understood.

Some monsters don't limp.

Some walk among us.

And sometimes, hidden behind a tale of horror, there is not vengeance—

but a heart that has longed for justice.

Chapter Fifteen

The Weight of Bones

In San Jacinto, a Colombian town nestled among endless plains and golden crops where tradition runs as deep as roots in fertile soil, the wind carried more than just the scent of damp earth when it swept down from the mountains. It brought with it a high, undulating whistle that would raise goosebumps on even the bravest soul—a sound that crept through every crack as if possessed of its own dark life. Though none had ever laid eyes upon the source of that haunting melody, every tongue in town spoke its name with the same hushed fear: El Silbón, The Whistler, the spectral figure said to roam these lands with his terrible burden of bones.

The humble, superstitious people of San Jacinto had their rituals of protection. Each evening, they would place glasses of aguardiente—that potent, anise-scented spirit whose very name meant "burning water"—upon their windowsills. With trembling hands, they drew crosses in ash upon their doors, renewing these sacred marks each night with still-warm cinders from their hearths, as if time itself might wear away their sheltering power. The bitter scent of burnt wood mingled with the cold night air, each cross both prayer and shield against the darkness.

But Víctor, the wealthiest man in the village, sneered at these ancient beliefs. His fortune was built on foundations of deceit and threat, mortared with the tears of those he'd wronged. The heartbroken wails of Manuel Herrera's widow still echoed through San Jacinto's dusty streets, a testament to the day Víctor's men had torn her from her ancestral land. Her young son had clung to the roots of a tree his grandfather had planted, his small hands gripping the rough bark as if trying to hold back the tide of injustice with nothing but the force of his desperate love.

That afternoon, standing in the village square, Víctor

raised high a bottle he'd stolen from a window marked with protective ash. Aguardiente splashed from its neck as he shook it in defiance of heaven and hell alike.

"I'm not afraid of El Silbón!" he roared, his voice thick with drink and his eyes blazing with dangerous pride. "Let him come, if he's man enough! I'll be waiting with my machete!"

From the shadow of the great ceiba—an ancient tree considered sacred throughout these lands, its sprawling canopy having witnessed generations of both injustice and resistance—a young boy with large, solemn eyes watched in silence. This was Mateo, who, though too young to fully grasp the weight of the adults' words, felt their impact like thunder in his bones.

Not waiting for nightfall to claim him, Mateo ran back to his grandfather Don Jerónimo's rancho, his bare feet sliding across the dry earth as if the ground itself urged him homeward. When he arrived, breathless and wide-eyed, the sun had begun its descent behind the plains, and an icy breeze whispered through the windows.

Inside the modest home, barely lit by the flickering dance of an oil lamp, Don Jerónimo calmly traced an ash cross on the door. The boy watched in reverent silence, his chest still heaving from his run, until he could no longer contain the question burning in his throat.

"Grandfather," he asked, his voice quavering, "is it true that El Silbón punishes the wicked? What if he mistakes me for Víctor?"

The old man set aside the tobacco he was rolling and lifted his gaze to his grandson. His eyes, though tired, held steady with the weight of untold stories.

"El Silbón isn't like us, boy," he said, his voice carrying that special kind of calm that frightens more than fear itself. "He's a warning to those who leave wounds in the earth and in people's hearts. They say he was once a proud man, so consumed by greed that he murdered his own father for money. His grandfather, destroyed by grief and rage, cursed him to wander eternally, carrying the bones of the life he took. Since then, his whistle has been an omen of doom for those who think themselves beyond the reach of justice."

Mateo swallowed hard and hugged his knees, curling up beside the warmth of the hearth.

"What if I hear him, Grandfather?" he whispered. "What should I do?"

Don Jerónimo exhaled a cloud of tobacco smoke, giving the words time to settle in the dim air.

"If you hear him close, he's far away," he said slowly. "But if he sounds distant..." He paused, each word hanging heavy in the air like morning mist. "Pray, because that means he's already upon you."

When night finally wrapped its dark arms around the village and the wind fell suddenly, unnaturally still, Víctor strode into the wilderness. He walked with his machete in hand and his chest swollen with arrogance. Each step took him further from the settlement, deeper into a darkness that seemed to devour everything in its path. Then he heard it.

A whistle.

At first, barely a whisper on the wind.

Then thin, sharp, so high-pitched it pierced his ears like a needle of ice.

He froze, the machete wavering in his trembling hand. He squeezed his eyes shut for a moment and whispered to himself: "It's far away… but if it sounds far away…"

When he opened his eyes, it was already too late. Among the shadows, he saw it: a tall, twisted figure with eyes that burned like dying embers and a sack slung over its shoulder that seemed to writhe with terrible life. The specter dropped its burden, and the bones that spilled forth arranged themselves one by one, forming the faces of those Víctor had wronged. Farmers, children, women. All watching him in eternal, accusing silence.

"These are the ones you stole from and humiliated," spoke a voice that seemed to emanate from the wind itself, as the night sank into a deep, raw silence—like the final sigh of something that dares not die.

They say in San Jacinto that each night, when the wind howls down from the mountains and El Silbón's whistle loses itself among the shadows, a hunched figure can be seen walking the village boundaries. No one approaches, but all bear witness: a man bent beneath an invisible weight, dragging his feet as if carrying the past of entire generations.

The elders say it's Víctor, condemned to walk the same paths traced by the tears of those he dispossessed. They've seen him pause before the fields he once stole, standing motionless while the earth blooms with white flowers at dawn. These delicate blooms, which no one dares touch for they're considered sacred, are said to be the earth's own offering of forgiveness to those who find the courage to face their guilt.

The children of San Jacinto no longer fear the whistle in the night. They've learned that true horror dwells not in the ghosts who carry bones, but in the living who walk unburdened by conscience. In their schoolroom, alongside multiplication tables and poets' verses, they learn that the earth holds memory, and that each ash cross their families draw upon their doors serves as both shield and promise of justice.

In San Jacinto, where the wind sings stories older than sorrow itself, justice is not merely a dream that fades with dawn. It's a seed planted deep in the hearts of those who dare to remember. And as long as there remains an elder drawing an ash cross with trembling hands, or a child gazing toward the horizon in search of a different future, the weight of bones will endure as a reminder—not of what they lost, but of the strength they found to endure it, while the wind keeps whispering stories that only the brave dare to hear.

Everyday Weapons

Silas Dakar

Dreams and Metaphors

Silas Dakar

Chapter Sixteen

Juan's Last Dream

The taste of the sea lingered on Juan's lips as a perpetual reminder of his identity. He was returning from another exhausting day, his net loaded more with disappointments than with fish, his hands weathered by years of battling the waves told stories his voice had never spoken.

As he secured his boat to the dock posts, a distant murmur caught his attention. A crowd was gathering around a figure who seemed to radiate his own light: a tall, slender man of middle age, whose smile had the power to disarm even the most cynical skeptic. He wore immaculate white clothes and spoke in a language that was as mysterious to Juan as the depths of the ocean. His childhood, consumed by the needs of the sea and survival, had not allowed him to know more of the world than what could be seen from his beach.

Driven by a curiosity he didn't even understand himself, Juan pushed his way through the crowd like someone swimming against the current. Upon reaching the speaker, he encountered a gaze that seemed to contain all the kindness of heaven. Intrigued, he looked among the followers for someone who could translate those enigmatic words. A man who introduced himself as Simon Peter explained, "The master speaks of universal love, peace among peoples, and the patience that heals the world's wounds. He teaches us that wealth should flow like water, reaching every corner thirsty for justice."

The master, with that intuition only true leaders possess, recognized something special in Juan: behind his melancholy lived a purity that rivaled that of angels. Through his disciple James the Younger, he delivered a message that would resonate in his heart: "Young fisherman, abandon your nets and join our cause. You will no longer fish for fish, but for souls." Like an invisible hook, those words caught Juan's spirit, and without hesitation, he decided to follow this new path.

His journey north was an awakening of the senses. The cliffs rose like guardians of an earthly paradise; crystal-clear rivers entoned melodies born from the heart's very core of the earth. Juan watched in wonder as the master's influence grew: every village, every town, every city they visited surrendered to his message. Language barriers faded in the face of the power of his words, which seemed to touch a universal truth in every heart that listened.

However, the south revealed the darkest face of the world: rivers carried the shame of pollution, forests whispered their agony in a harrowing silence, lands had forgotten how to give life. But even there, amidst the rawest misery, the master's message found fertile ground in souls hungry for hope.

Gradually, Juan unraveled the mysteries of that language that seemed to open all doors. But when they arrived at the master's homeland, something changed. The cities stood like monuments to power, and the discourse that had so captivated him underwent a disturbing metamorphosis. No longer was there talk of universal love or social justice; now the words revolved around expanding dominance, the need for protection, and military strengthening.

Sadness seeped into Juan's heart like salty water into an open wound. The scent of the sea beckoned him more strongly than ever; he longed for the rhythmic rocking of his boat, the steadfast loyalty of his anchor, and the unwavering certainty of his compass. He longed for his father's worn smile, his brother's house where sand crept through every crack, his mother's voice that seemed to sway the air like a lullaby.

"This fishing for men is not for me," he thought as he walked away through the wide avenues of that rigid city. Amid the deafening bustle of the crowd, he heard the master's voice one last time: "Make America Great Again."

Juan smiled bitterly: it didn't matter the language or the land, all saviors ended up preaching the same sermon. Then he realized that some dreams, like elusive fish, are best left gliding freely through the boundless sea of memory.

Chapter Seventeen

Julián's Dream

The roar of machines was the constant music in Julián's life. For fifteen years, he had worked in that factory where time was measured in metallic clangs and grinding gears. The workers' sweat mixed with the oil dripping from hungry machines, while the suffocating heat turned each breath into a deliberate struggle. Julián knew every sound, every vibration, like a father distinguishes the breathing of his sleeping child.

Pedro, his shift partner for a decade, used to say that the factory was a beast that fed on their lives. "Look at my hands, Julián," he would say, showing his calloused fingers marked with scars. "Each scar marks a day when the beast craved more of us." With five children at home, Pedro saw in those marks the price he paid to support them.

During night shifts, when the outside world slept, Julián observed the mechanical dance of pistons and pulleys from his post on the assembly line. He watched as Manuel, the youngest on the shift, struggled to keep up with production's relentless pace. The new ones always started like this: frightened, overwhelmed by the monster that never rested. Few lasted more than a month.

During rare breaks, Julián would take refuge in a secluded corner of the cafeteria, where the noise became a distant echo. There he would take out a worn notebook from his overalls pocket and draw. These weren't simple doodles; they were detailed plans for a different factory. Industrial fans to combat the heat, guards to protect workers' hands, rest areas illuminated by natural light. Each design was born from a need he had witnessed, from shared pain.

The change began on a humid summer night. Exhausted after a double shift, Manuel put his hand in the hydraulic press a second before it came down. His scream cut through the factory like lightning. Luckily, it was only two broken fingers, but it could have been all. It could have been his dream of being a guitarist. It could have been his life.

That same night, Julián took out his notebook and began to write. It wasn't a simple complaint but a detailed manifesto backed by years of observation. Each page contained a problem and its solution; each paragraph carried the urgency of someone who had seen too much suffering.

"Are you crazy, Julián?" Pedro whispered when he showed him the letter, his face divided between fear and hope. "With five mouths to feed, I can't risk losing this."

"We already lost Torres and Ramírez last month," Manuel interjected from his chair, his bandaged fingers a silent reminder. "How many more have to fall?"

"The machines are devouring us alive," Julián responded, folding the letter with determination. "What do you prefer, Pedro? To die in silence or stand up and live?"

The letter faced obstacles in management's hallways, but the seed was already planted. In the factory's dark corners, among steam and noise, workers started coming together, united by shared dreams of dignity. Julián's words resonated with those who, like him, dreamed of a better life.

The threat of a strike was the first blow. Media coverage was the second. Management, cornered between bad publicity and possible government intervention, began to yield. First, they installed safety guards, and then ventilation was improved. Shifts were shortened, and break areas were transformed into more human spaces. The beast was beginning to be tamed.

Ten years later, Julián observed the factory from across the street. The building still stood, but something had changed. He saw robotic arms moving with millimetric precision through the windows, tireless and efficient. Where there were once tired but human faces, now there were screens and sensors. His old position was occupied by a machine that never complained, dreamed, or imagined a better world.

Pedro passed by his side, carrying a grocery bag. He no longer worked in the factory; none of the old crew did.

"You know what's ironic, Julián?" he said with a sad smile. "We fought for more human conditions and ended up being replaced by machines that don't need conditions at all."

Julián nodded silently. The muffled roar of the automated factory echoed like a mocking metallic laugh. In his pocket, the old notebook of dreams weighed like a tombstone.

"We won our rights," he muttered, "but lost our jobs."

The robots' lights kept blinking behind the windows, indifferent to dignity or rights, endlessly executing the work that once belonged to men who dared to dream of something better.

Chapter Eighteen

The Train of Dreams

(To Lucas Dakar, my brother, for all the stories born between tracks and stations, for the trains that saw us grow, and for those still waiting at some forgotten waystation.)

In the village, where nights were as long as silences, something inexplicable happened as darkness fell. The Train of Dreams would appear in the heart of the old abandoned tracks. It passed every night at the same hour, its distant whistle crossing the air like an echo from the past, announcing its arrival with a spectral glow in its carriages. They said those who boarded the train could relive a crucial moment from their past, but that gift came shrouded in shadows, with a cost only the soul could calculate.

Lucas, a man laden with silences and voids, had heard stories about the train since childhood. But the train's whisper began to call him when Memín, his best friend, was lost in the shadows of an unsettled conflict. One night, regret pressing against his chest, he decided to board.

The first time, the train took him to that fateful afternoon. He relived every word spoken and unspoken, every gesture that now weighed on him like a chain. He changed the outcome, but upon returning to the present, he felt the relief was fleeting. The pain of the past had mutated into something different but equally sharp.

He boarded the train again, this time to face a wound with his father. Upon returning, he discovered that the weight of that new memory didn't replace the previous one but added to it as if the train showed him that pain is a constant that transforms but never dissipates.

Finally, one night, as the train approached with its characteristic roar, Luca stopped at the platform and observed the lights illuminating the empty carriages. He understood that the past, no matter how much he rewrote it, only brought new forms of pain that would never completely abandon him. With a deep sigh, Lucas let the train continue its journey without him. "No more, to hell with the rails," he let it escape like an incantation fading into the void while the echo of the whistle faded into the night.

At dawn, Luca walked toward the village with a strange relief. He had decided to stay in the present, accepting that pain is a fellow traveler but never the journey's end. From then on, the Train of Dreams continued to appear, but for Lucas, its whistle was no longer a call but a reminder that, sometimes, true peace lies in learning to live with the scars that forged us.

Chapter Nineteen

Faith In Uncertainty

The basement of the old church smelled of dampness and secrets. Ernesto watched the shadows of his companions cast on the stone walls, wondering if his doubts were a betrayal or the most honest form of loyalty. Manuel, the group's leader, spoke of justice and revolution with the confidence of a proph-et, while the candles drew halos on the peeling walls.

"The victory is near," Manuel proclaimed, his words echoing among the ancient arches. "The peo-ple will awaken."

"And when will the people awaken?" Ernesto asked, raising his gaze. "Because I've heard those words my entire life, and nothing changes."

Manuel paused, his furrowed brow casting a shadow over the walls.

"Do you doubt our cause, Ernesto?" he replied firmly.

"I don't doubt the cause," Ernesto answered. "I doubt us, our methods. What if we're just perpet-uating a cycle?"

The silence that followed was as thick as fog. The candles flickered, and an uncomfortable mur-mur spread through the basement.

"Doubt is a luxury of cowards," sneered Ricardo, the youngest and most fervent. "If you can't be-lieve, then leave."

Julia, who had remained silent, emerged from the shadows with a lit cigarette.

"Doubt," she said, exhaling a cloud of smoke, "is the only path to truth. My brother doubted too, and his doubts guided him to his last breath."

Everyone turned to her. Julia sat down next to Ernesto, her voice soft but filled with determina-tion.

"The night before they killed him, he told me: 'I'd rather die doubting than live believing lies.'"

In the weeks that followed, Ernesto's doubts transformed. They were no longer chains that para-lyzed him but compasses guiding him toward deeper questions. At each meeting, while others shout-ed slogans, he learned to listen to the silences between the words.

On the night of the final action, when everyone was ready to move, Ernesto stood up.

"Perhaps we don't have all the answers," he said, looking each of his companions in the eye, "but it's better to doubt while standing than to live on your knees."

Julia smiled from her corner. After all, the revolution didn't need blind believers but souls willing to question."

Chapter Twenty

The Wind's Fragments

The wind carried secrets that only Lia seemed to notice, perhaps because she kept one herself: her mother's absence, who had drifted away like just another leaf in the autumn wind, leaving behind only the echo of unfulfilled promises. Since then, every lost paper she found tangled in branches or spinning between stones seemed like a message searching for its destiny, like the last words she had never heard.

She collected them carefully and kept them in a carved wooden box by her bed, an heirloom from her mother. Some were white as winter's first breath, others yellowed like ancient parchments, and some bore soft hues, as if they had absorbed the light of dawn or dusk. Each paper, Lia thought, carried a fragment of life, an interrupted story that deserved to be preserved.

One breezy afternoon, the capricious wind led her to a hill where a forgotten tower stood. Its spiral windows seemed to watch over the horizon, and the air whispered through its cracks like voices calling out. Lia felt a shiver but let her curiosity guide her.

The wooden door groaned as it opened, revealing an interior bathed in the golden light of sunset. In the center, surrounded by shelves that reached the vaulted ceiling, an old man carefully examined papers with the patience of a watchmaker inspecting delicate gears. The shelves were organized by color: blues like tears, whites like unspoken sighs, yellows like withered memories, and reds like burning promises.

When Lia stepped inside, a floorboard creaked beneath her feet. The old man looked up and offered a brief smile like sunlight breaking through clouds after the rain.

"Why do you keep so many messages?" she asked softly.

The old man picked up a lavender-colored piece of paper and ran his knotted fingers over its surface as if deciphering a hidden language.

""Because each one is a fragment of a soul, little collector," he replied, soft and worn by time. "Like you, I know some need to wander before finding their place."

Lia pulled a pink paper from her pocket. "And what if they never reach where they're meant to go?"

The old man's eyes held the depth of many lifetimes.

"Nothing said to the wind is ever lost. Sometimes, the message isn't for who we think, but for the one who needs to find it."

Lia frowned, her fingers nervously twisting the hem of her sweater.

"How do you know if it reaches the right person?"

The old man rose with calm deliberation and walked toward a spiral window. The sunset light gilded his hair.

"Come," he said, offering her a blank paper. "Write something and see for yourself."

With trembling but resolute hands, Lia wrote: "I'm here. Can you hear me? I miss you every day." She climbed the stone steps to the highest window, where the wind was strongest, and released the paper.

She watched it rise, dance in the air, and shimmer in the last rays of sunlight until it disappeared into the horizon ablaze with fire and gold.

"And now?" she asked, turning to the old man, her eyes glistening with unshed tears.

"Now," he said with a serene smile, "listen."

The wind grew stronger, making the papers on the shelves rustle like ancient voices. Amidst those murmurs, Lia thought she heard something familiar—a voice she remembered from her dreams: "I always hear you, my little collector of stories."

That night, upon returning home, she opened her carved wooden box. One by one, she released the papers she had kept for so long. She watched them drift into the moonlit sky, each glowing like a fleeting spark in the darkness.

The last paper she released was the exact color of her mother's eyes. She watched it rise and, for a moment, it seemed to form the silhouette of an embrace before vanishing into the starlit night.

From then on, Lia continued to find lost papers, but she no longer kept them. She read them, released them, and on some afternoons climbed the tower to share cinnamon tea with the old man. Together, they watched the messages dance in the wind, carrying incomplete stories toward unseen destinations.

"Sometimes," the old man had told her, "letting go is the only way to find it." Lia finally understood that some stories must remain unfinished so others can write their ending.

Everyday Weapons

Silas Dakar

About the Author

Silas Dakar is a writer and essayist dedicated to examining the human condition with a balance of analytical rigor and evocative storytelling. His work explores power, identity, and social transformation, connecting historical perspectives to the present. Whether through reflective essays or immersive short stories, Dakar invites readers to uncover new perspectives on the complexities of the world and their place in it.

www.ingramcontent.com/pod-product-compliance
Lightning Source LLC
LaVergne TN
LVHW092053060526
838201LV00047B/1369